Tales at Twilight

Scaredy Finds His Courage

By Abigail Carr

Deep in the forest, in a small, brambly den,
A forest cat had made his home.
Unlike the other cats that lived in these woods,
He was too scared to explore or to roam.

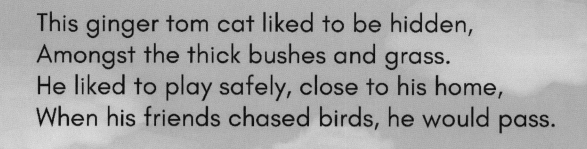

This ginger tom cat liked to be hidden,
Amongst the thick bushes and grass.
He liked to play safely, close to his home,
When his friends chased birds, he would pass.

Being so fearful, nervous and worried,
Scaredy Cat became his name.
Afraid of almost everything,
It really was a shame.

He would run, leap or dash, away in a flash,
From the spiders spinning webs in the trees.
He would scream at the sight of the tiniest mite,
Or even from his own itchy fleas.

When the sky was at its darkest in the middle of the night,
And the nighttime noises grew louder,
Even a swoosh of his own tail would give him a fright,
And he'd hide behind the nearest tall flower.

But there came a time when Scaredy Cat felt
That enough was about enough!
He really must conquer his fears and become,
A forest cat that can be tough.

He set out one day with a goal in his mind
To try to stop being so scared.
As he trotted along under tall trees,
"I will be brave!", he declared.

He tried not to think of what was under his feet,
As he trampled through damp, auburn leaves.
"Are there bugs, are there grubs crawling down there?"
"I don't want to see them please!"

After some time Scaredy suddenly stopped,
And his ears twitched as he listened in fear.
Something was under the leaves on the ground,
What was that sound he could hear?

Scratchity, scratch, scratch, scratchity scratch!
Rippity, rippity rip!
Scaredy's legs started shaking, his body went still,
He had a quivering lip.

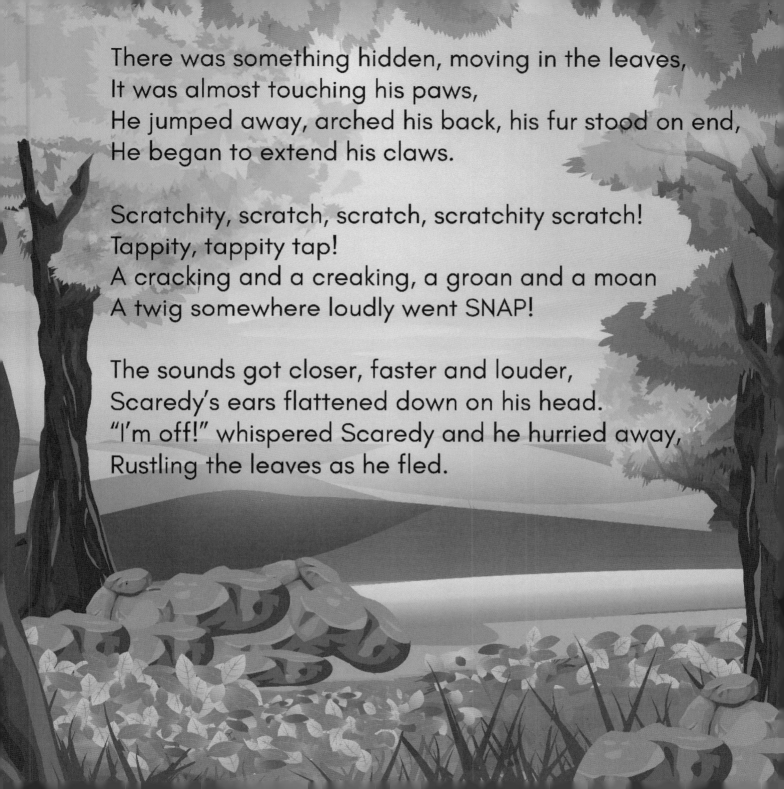

There was something hidden, moving in the leaves,
It was almost touching his paws,
He jumped away, arched his back, his fur stood on end,
He began to extend his claws.

Scratchity, scratch, scratch, scratchity scratch!
Tappity, tappity tap!
A cracking and a creaking, a groan and a moan
A twig somewhere loudly went SNAP!

The sounds got closer, faster and louder,
Scaredy's ears flattened down on his head.
"I'm off!" whispered Scaredy and he hurried away,
Rustling the leaves as he fled.

Just then a brown figure leapt up high in the air,
Out of the leaves and the mud.
"Aagh! Oh no! What's that!" shouted Scaredy,
Then he heard a gentle thud.

Looking over to where all the commotion had been,
He stopped running, turned back, then he smiled.
It was Brownie the Cat, his friend, she was playing,
She was so excited and wild.

"Brownie! You scared me!" Scaredy Cat called
"You were hidden in the leaves on the ground"
"What were you doing there, waiting to pounce?"
"You were making a very strange sound!"

"Oh, Scaredy I'm sorry", purred Brownie with a grin,
"I was looking for some insects to chase"
"Insects!" exclaimed Scaredy, "No thank you very much,"
"Let's get out of this place!"

Scaredy felt better as they walked on together,
So, he waved his long tail in the air.
The afternoon sun shone through the trees,
Casting long shadows here and there.

Just ahead, there was something odd in the trees,
It really was quite out of place.
A long, black shadow was moving this way and that,
At an extremely fast pace.

Flickity, flick, flick, flickity flick!
Shakety, shakety, shake!
Across, up and down, then around and around,
It moved like a long, angry snake.

Scaredy didn't move, he didn't want see,
Though he watched from the corner of his eye.
He was terrified to go any further along,
In case it slithered close by.

Whippity, whip, whip, whippity, whip!
Swishity, swishity, swish!
Scaredy right now just wanted to go home,
Oh, that was his very big wish.

As he saw the dark shadow hook and curl round,
The thick branch above his head
"I don't like that shadow moving up there,"
"It looks like something dangerous!" he said

Brownie glanced up, then quickly climbed up the tree,
And disappeared right into the shade.
Scaredy tried to see his friend through the leaves,
Now he was extremely afraid.

"Scaredy Cat!", came Brownie's giggly meow,
And a wave of her little brown paw.
"It's just Tux, our good friend, he's playing up here,"
"It was his tail hanging down that you saw"

Tux looked down, beaming and said,
"Hey Scaredy, come up and play!"
"These branches are great for sharpening your claws,"
"You're welcome up here any day."

Not a snake! Scaredy thought, what brilliant news,
Though that tree is so very tall.
If he climbed on the branch to have a good scratch,
He thought he would surely fall.

"No thank you!", he said "I'm happy down here",
With my feet firmly on the ground.
Now as they talked, the daylight was fading,
And that was when Scaredy found,

That he was standing alone on the path of the forest,
And day was slowly turning to night.
The other cats saw Scaredy's face looking worried,
"We'll come down to you, it's alright!"

The three cats hurried along the path all together,
As the sun went behind the hill.
Scaredy calmed down little by little,
With his friends by his side, until...

A drop of water splashed onto Scaredy's pink nose,
Then another onto the tip of his ear.
He knew what was happening and what was to come,
They would get wet if they stayed out here.

Splashity splash, splash, splashity splash!
Ploppity, ploppity plop!
Huge drops of rain fell all around,
It didn't seem likely to stop.

"Aagh!" shouted Brownie and Tux both together,
"We don't like the rain one bit!"
They looked here and there, they wanted some shelter,
But there was nowhere undercover to sit.

Splattery, splat, splat, splattery splat!
Swashity, swashity swash!
Brownie's fur was all scruffy, dirty and wet,
Tux jumped in a puddle, splish splosh!

"What shall we do? We just want to be dry,
But it's only stones and rocks around here."
The rocks! That's it, Scaredy thought suddenly,
He had just had a brilliant idea.

"Follow me!" he called, as he dashed onto the rocks,
"There is a place we can go up there."
Shelter, on the rocks? Thought the other cats confused,
But right now, they didn't much care.

They followed behind Scaredy, running to keep up,
To their surprise he climbed higher and higher.
Close to the top, he pointed out a small cave,
"If we go in, we will surely be drier."

But this dark cave was not at all empty,
There was something large and hairy in there.
Two huge, bright green eyes shone through the gloom,
With an eerie, unblinking stare.

Tux crept along with his tummy down low,
Brownie stayed back, now trying to hide
But, Scaredy Cat wasn't afraid this time,
He just ran over and straight inside.

The rain beat down faster and the wind picked up speed,
The cave was the only place they could go.
They peered inside, "Scaredy?", they said,
But all they heard was their own echo.

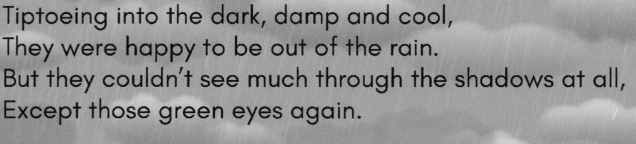

Tiptoeing into the dark, damp and cool,
They were happy to be out of the rain.
But they couldn't see much through the shadows at all,
Except those green eyes again.

Coming much closer now, larger and wider,
They could see sharp, white teeth too!
The two cats crouched down with their paws over their eyes,
"Scaredy Cat, where are you?"

But after a moment it wasn't so dark anymore,
And slowly they began to see,
The oval green eyes belonged to a cat,
"This is Rocky", Scaredy was smiling with glee.

A grey-speckled, old cat, a friendly smile on his face,
Stood there joyfully chuckling.
He gave them each a little pat on the head,
"Welcome young cats, come in"

Brownie and Tux sighed with relief
And began to try and get dry.
Now they were calmer, and had time to think,
They couldn't help wondering why.

"Scaredy, why were you so fearless just now?",
Brownie asked, cleaning rain from her back.
"Yes!", Tux agreed, "these rocks are so high,
"And this cave is oh so black."

"Well!" said Scaredy, "I like to play in the rain,
"Quite unlike any usual cat"
"You needed my help to find a dry place,"
"It was my time to be bold, like that."

"I knew I could help you if I brought you up here,"
"As Rocky is an old friend of mine."
"Besides, when I'm with you, I feel braver than ever,"
"Like a real forest feline!"

The four cats now huddled closer together,
As the rain slowly came to a stop.
The sun was way down and twilight had fallen,
Around the tree-lined hilltop.

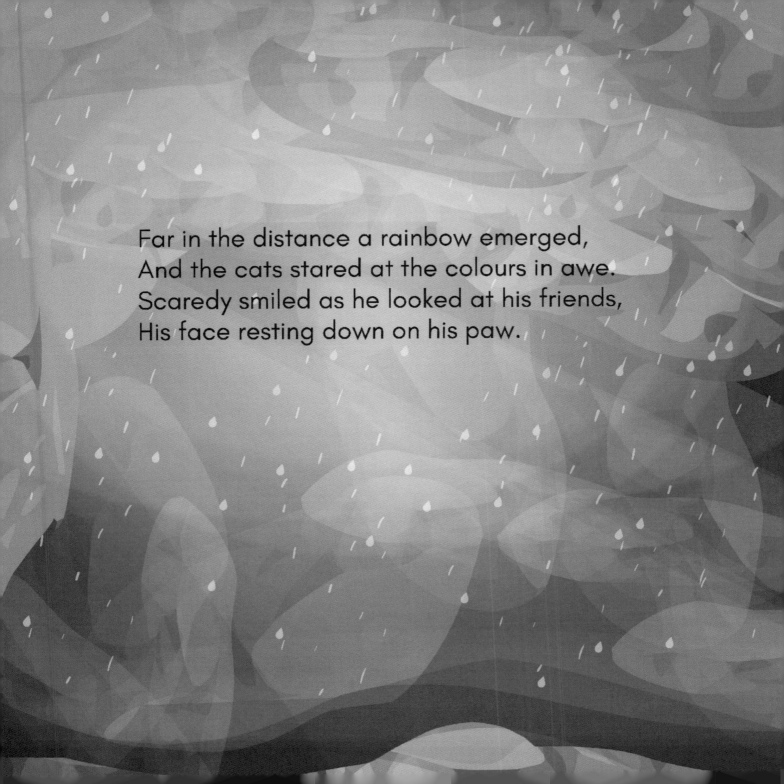

Far in the distance a rainbow emerged,
And the cats stared at the colours in awe.
Scaredy smiled as he looked at his friends,
His face resting down on his paw.

Scratchity, scratch, scratch, scratchity scratch!
Tappity, tappity tap!
The cats jumped up and looked all around,
They cried out together "What's that?"

About the Author

Abigail Carr has specialised in teaching in Early Childhood Education and Care for 26 years. She has taught, managed, and led the establishment of 10 kindergartens in Hong Kong.

Since the Covid-19 pandemic, Abigail has worked closely with mums of children under 8 years old, taking them from anxious and unsure about their child's behaviour and learning, to connected and trusting of the processes that they can take to positively influence their child's moral character and academic outcomes. Abigail also helps teachers and schools provide the operational school culture, the pedagogy and the staff professional development required to maximise the learning outcomes of children in early years classrooms.

Underpinning all she does for children, families, schools, and teachers is the belief that emphasising relationships and social-emotional development is paramount to academic success.

Tales at Twilight was born of many a walk in the Hong Kong countryside. Abigail has watched the hills come alive with amazing Asian animals as dusk falls each evening. It is her belief that if children are raised knowing that they are a part of nature, and loving every aspect of the natural world around them, they will grow to care so much about planet Earth, they will be able to save it.

Associated home learning and kindergarten curriculum documents for Tales at Twilight are available on Abigail's website www.theearlyyearsspecialist.com.

"Scaredy Finds His Courage" is Abigail's first children's book.

Connect with Abigail:
Website: theearlyyearsspecialist.com
Instagram: @earlyyears_specialist and @ece_educators
Facebook: The Calm Parent Space (group) The Confident Early Childhood Educator (group)

Printed in Great Britain
by Amazon

34305686R00021